Letter from Teplice

Annabella Baker

Disclaimer

LETTER FROM TEPLICE

To my grandfather Guido, who left too soon

Acknowledgments

My gratitude is going to my dear husband for his patience and support throughout the long evenings and nights spent writing.

Thanks to Oscar, my wonderful friend, whom as always, is my first critic and the only one able to read my notes in every language I may write them.

Many thanks to my cousin RF. He knows why.

Table of Contents

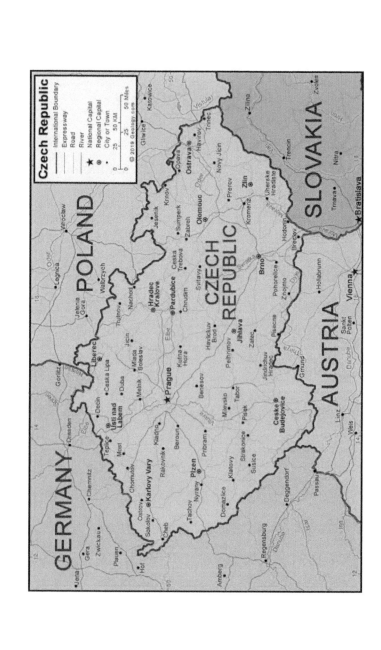

"Hope is not the conviction that something will turn out well, but the certainty that something makes sense, regardless of how it turns out."
— Václav Havel

Introduction

Lottie works as receptionist in a very elegant hotel in Berlin Kreuzberg. She grew up in Vienna. She loves black and white photographs.

I had the opportunity to meet her a few times.

She promised herself to be happy, to live life to the full, to leave behind any sadness. Instead, she lives in a constant of hope and despair.

Blue eyed and beautiful, she lives with her adorable dog, and a heavy secret. That secret kept her going.

There is Prague in winter, Teplice and a letter. She will need to read that letter on her own.

She's wearing his jumper nearly every night. He told her to forget Teplice. Then there is that smell of eucalyptus and cigarette.

You can meet her through these pages. The book in your hands is her story.

1

"Si levano a corona,le ininterrotte catene dei monti che si profilano maestose e possenti,sullo sfondo del cielo."

"The uninterrupted chains of the mountains rise as a crown, majestic and mighty, against the background of the sky."

-Nini Franzellin

18th December, Berlin

The sky looked hazy after a snowy night on a typical winter day. There was snow on the silent cobbled street, but Mitzi, the chunky, yellow Labrador, jumped in it anyway. She was digging until she touched muddy wet soil and continued to dig just a little more. Lottie, who stood a few meters away, knows full well that her coat would be dirty, and there was no point in dissuading her from that exciting adventure.

Muddy dog, happy dog.

They were both clearly having a good time, having just come back from their usual Saturday walk and resting at their preferred place, under the linden trees, not far from their apartment. After a small break, they continued a few more steps to reach home.

Once they entered the building, Lottie paused to feel the warmth, when suddenly, a smell brought a thought to her mind. It wasn't like the thought was an unknown one. She got it from time to time, and the reaction was always the same.

She quickly brushed it away and proceeded towards the letterbox. She had only been there a couple of months, but there were envelopes already. She smiled. The effectiveness of the postal system gave her a sense of reliability.

These days, she took all the consistency and reliability she needed from the small things.

There were too many aspects in life that couldn't be controlled; so, she compensated herself with the things that didn't change through the years.

She stepped into the elevator, holding the envelopes but not having looked at any of them.

She loved her new flat, which was in a tall building that stood with other tall buildings in an old, cobbled street. The building was historical, standing proudly and fearlessly in that neighborhood of Berlin. She had always been curious about it and wondered what the story behind it was, but she had refrained from actively searching for the answer to her question because she was trying to prove Ingrid, her best friend, wrong. So instead, she cast her mind back to what Ingrid had said when she first visited, a beaming smile spreading across her face.

"I bet you've been to the library, searching for the history of this place!" Ingrid laughed.

"No, not yet, and you never know, maybe I won't," Lottie responded.

"Like you could ever control yourself when it comes to such things!"

"I can," Lottie boasted, even though she wasn't sure she believed it herself.

They had laughed about it, and Lottie had made up her mind that she would not go searching for the history of the old building, even if the temptation was high.

The elevator stopped at the 4th and last floor. Her stomach rumbled as she walked out of it, with Mitzi in front of her. Lottie was hungry, but she was determined to wait for Ingrid. They had planned to have lunch together.

She was grateful that Ingrid only lived two streets away. She had moved to Berlin a few years previously, and now Lottie had finally decided to relocate as well. It was a new city for Lottie, with its history and unique style.

Lottie was always searching for something better that kept her mind occupied, away from her thoughts and secrets that, year after year, became harder and harder to keep. She didn't like to talk about it. It was a part of her life that she wanted to forget because of the helpless sadness that would envelop her each time she even thought about it.

Berlin was vastly different from the world where everything reminded her of him; his laughter, his smile, and his soft voice.

"I'm over that now. I'm moving on," she said to herself. It was what she had been saying to herself for months now. Sometimes it worked, at other times she found there were too many emotions to overcome before getting to that place of peace.

Moving to Berlin, away from home, had also helped her stay away from a lot of her grief.

She walked into her white-painted apartment, the smell of fresh paint was still so strong.

She grabbed the towel that she kept near the door and started to give Mitzi a bit of a rubdown. She glared back at her with big, cute eyes as Lottie kissed her on her big nose in response. Walking over to the large bow window, she looked down into the street; most of her view was blocked by the branches of the tall, beautiful linden trees that stood right below.

It reminded her of that nostalgic past from which she wanted to turn a page, to safeguard herself, her mind, and, indeed, her heart.

The top of Friedrichstrasse at the junction with Unter den Linden was the perfect compromise.

Everything was just how she liked it. The distance from the metro, the shops, the hotel where she was working, the Tiergarten where she loved to take Mitzi for their walks, and the café where she could meet up with Ingrid.

Today was just another typical day. She threw the keys on the kitchen table next to the oranges that she didn't even like but kept because it was fashionable to have a fruit bowl. What's a fruit bowl without oranges in it, anyway? She tossed the stack of envelopes on the green sofa just a little away from where she stood at the entrance.

Then, next to the radiator, she removed her shoes and hung her jacket on grandma's old rack.

A chalkboard was to her far-left stating:

To buy	To do
Äpfel	Lunch with Ingrid 1 pm
Käse, Butter	Freitag 10 Uhr Veterinary

She smiled at the chalkboard. A bit of everything. Lists and reminders in a mix of English and German. She sat down and cuddled her gorgeous yellow labrador, who had followed her to the sofa, just like she followed her everywhere.

She got Mitzi when she was eight weeks old and had never let her go since.

Mitzi was her world, perhaps even her one true love.

She'd had other dogs in the past, but there was no doubt that she felt most passionate about Mitzi. Not even her fun and loyal crossbreed Tobias had a place this huge in her heart. She had only been a child when she got him as a birthday present. Lottie had just turned 8, and Tobias had been a present from grandad. Her parents weren't sure about the idea, but she had already decided he would stay with her forever.

Her "forever" lasted only six years. He died far too soon, leaving her with a huge hole in her heart.

She snapped out of her thoughts and turned away from the chalkboard. She knew what was about to happen.

"I did not travel all this way, change the city and create a whole new life only to feel sorry for myself," she thought.

She reached for the mail and started to go through it to see if there was anything urgent or important. She flipped through each envelope one after the other.

Bills, bills....

There didn't seem to be much of any importance. Just bills as usual.

Who would have thought moving and changing city would be so expensive? Mitzi looked in her direction from the warm, comfortable sofa where she was lying.

Then suddenly, that buzzing in her ears returned, as did the dizziness. The noise from the busy road downstairs was gone; Mitzi let out a low whine, a plaintiff request for food.

Looking through the envelopes, Lottie's hand started to tremble as her gaze fell upon one envelope in particular. All other envelopes fell to the floor, as an unmistakable silence suddenly surrounded her, one which she was far too familiar with.

The handwriting. It was etched in her memory. Forever would be.

Proud and elegant handwriting. She knew the narrow "O", she recognized that stretched "L."

Those long letters tapered like his fingers.

She knew exactly where that envelope had come from, and she knew who had written it. She froze. She'd been waiting for it for nearly 15 years.

"15 years!" she whispered.

"Nein! Nein! Warum?"

When she got angry, she would always shout in German, which was much easier. It came more naturally. At the end of the day, she was born and bred in Austria, or as she proudly said to her friends, she was born in the grandeur of Vienna.

Memories filled her mind. She closed her eyes, and she was taken back into that garden she knew so well.

He takes her hand, leading her through the garden while his voice continues to tell her a story. She can hear his voice high up; he is a tall man. He still stands six feet into the sky, but her best moments are when they both stay silent, just admiring the flowers, the sky, and everything that belongs to their dreams.

"You know, plants are a great medicine. There are special plants that help us heal, help us grow, and the knowledge of those plants is what we need."

She inherited the love for botany and flowers from him. He had a little workshop with all his bottles, infuses, and vases. She had always been so creative in arranging the flowers in the entrance hall of the hotel where she works.

Now, this letter in her hands is not what she expected ... or wanted. Not like this, anyway.

She'd been thinking about this moment for a while, but she never thought it would happen like this. Ever since that first day, she had dreamt of a completely different scenario. She had a whole play out in her head about what this day would look and feel like. How she would find out... find him.

"This is not fair. I wanted it to be a special day," she said to herself silently.

She brought the envelope close to her nostrils. She closed her eyes, inhaled deeply, taking in as much part of him as possible.

That smell. Eucalyptus and cigarettes.

She could almost see him holding the pen with his trembling, fragile hand.

His beautiful pale hands, those hands that had been holding hers so many times as they crossed the Opernring, climbing the Alps, strolling in between the stalls of the busy Christmas market in Rathausplatz and so scared to lose her.

Allowing the scent to open the eyes of her memories, she knew in that moment it was him. Of course it was him.

She knew exactly who would leave that trail of scents on a letter. Her heart swelled with a feeling, however it wasn't what she had always expected to feel. She had expected joy, happiness, and excitement. It wasn't just those emotions that she felt, but rather a whirlwind. At that moment, she could hear his voice, see his eyes and smell all the plants and flowers that had left their lasting scent on his clothes and hair. She fought the tears.

"I was OK until 11.55.....Not anymore."

She looked around the room.

"I need to call Ingrid. I need to cancel our lunch. I can't go out like this," she thought to herself as she started to search for her phone. Just minutes before she walked into her apartment, she had noted that she was hungry. Now she wasn't even sure she would be able to keep any food down.

A few seconds later, her phone began to ring, and she finally located it. It was Ingrid.

She hesitated. She cleared her throat and tried to sound as normal as possible.

"Hey, Ingrid!" she said, masking her emotions.

"I'm downstairs...come on, let's go, I'm hungry."

Lottie froze.

She couldn't go out like this. She couldn't let anyone see her like this. Ingrid knew parts of her life, but she wanted time, no... she *needed* time to process.

She wanted to be alone with her thoughts and allow herself to soak in the new information and read the letter alone.

Her hands trembled slightly.

"I hate to let her down, and I can't hide. She knows me too well," Lottie thought to herself.

"Come up!"

"Why? Bist du nicht bereit?" Ingrid asked.

She sensed the tone in Lottie's voice almost immediately.

"Just come upstairs," she said, as she tried to fix her face, trying not to appear worried or tearful. She rushed to the mirror and dabbed at her eyes, but it didn't do much for the redness.

"OK, OK." It was clear in Ingrid's voice that she knew something had happened.

She knew Lottie well, very well. They had talked about this before, and she had even teased Lottie about it a couple of times.

"Now, you better have a good reason for dragging me up here," Ingrid said as she pushed Lottie's door open. She had barely finished what she was saying when she paused and looked at her friend at the door. "What happened, Lottie? Tell me!" she rushed out her words all at once.

But Lottie, instead, nodded at the envelope in her hand.

"Do you see this letter? The brown envelope and the handwriting." Ingrid looked at the envelope and then at her friend, eyes filled with intrigue.

"What are you talking about?" Ingrid asked with a frown.

Lottie opened her mouth to explain but suddenly found herself lost for words. Her mind was filled with memories, and tears welled up in her eyes.

Ingrid threw her arms around her friend.

"Sorry, Ingrid, this is so hard. Do you mind if I see you tomorrow?" Lottie finally managed to say. "Today, I just...I just can't," she stammered, tears pushing down her face in an unstoppable stream.

Ingrid looked at her friend's blue eyes sparkling like gems.

"Are you ok?" It was a weird question, it was obvious that Lottie was not okay, but it was also a loaded question. Was Lottie going to be okay if Ingrid left at that moment?

"Please, let's talk tomorrow."

"Tell me .... You know you can tell me everything."

"Please, Ingrid ..."

"Ja sicher, bis morgen Lottie."

Lottie looked down as more tears fell from her rosy, red cheeks, as the two girls collided in a warm embrace.

"Look, I'll come by and see you tomorrow, okay? Get some rest," Ingrid said as she knelt down to give Mitzi a kiss and headed out the door.

Lottie sighed a deep breath.

She knew her past and present very well, and up until that very moment, she thought she knew her future too.

With her back against the wall, staring at the bareness of her flat, she realized that was no longer the case. Her dreamlike, empty stare was interrupted as she realized that Mitzi was staring at her, tail wagging.

"Oh, sorry, my girl. I'll feed you now."

As Mitzi devoured her lunch, Lottie watched her eat, before returning to staring at the bare wall. She hadn't filled it with any paintings, as they were meant to arrive soon with the removal company from Vienna.

She had only moved to Berlin recently, thinking that she would be able to start a new life there, but how could she? At the end of the day, she had all those memories that followed her.

She wasn't ready to let them go.

She wore his jumper nearly every evening.

Photos of him were everywhere, on her phone, and in her mind.

She kept the cards with which they were playing because it was the last thing he touched and held.

Without asking, her parents had thrown away his last clothes and other belongings; breaking her heart for the second time.

She didn't speak to them for nearly a year after that.

Why keep the belongings of a dead man?

She remembered that pale afternoon a few years back when her father said to her,

"Darling, you need to let go of him now. There's no point holding on for so long."

She had shaken her head without even looking back at him.

"No," she said quietly, like a whisper.

"He died 10 years ago. Please, for your peace, try to let it go."

She continued to shake her head, her body automatically responding to the resistance of tears. To a considerable extent, she did know her father was right. But she refused to believe it. She knew deep within her that he was somewhere. It was kind of hard to explain to anyone. How would she explain now that the man in question was Johann, her grandfather?

He had disappeared about 15 years earlier.

And here she was, an adult woman still holding onto the belief that an older man would be alive somewhere. She was just waiting for him to send her a piece of information.

"I know it's hard, but I'm telling you because I don't want to see you suffer. I know you were very close to him."

"We weren't JUST close. He was my world," she said as her voice cracked, tears rolling down her face, tears of pain and frustration from all the days she had to live without him.

"I want him back! Now! I cry every day, everything reminds me of him!"

"He is dead. Lottie, get over it and get over yourself. He was my father."

"He's not dead!" she shouted.

He took a good look at her and shrugged his shoulders. He knew he had done his best, but at this point, he didn't quite understand her denial anymore.

They put it down to grief.

They didn't know. Nobody else knew the promises the two of them had made to each other.

After all, he told her all his secrets, and she wouldn't dare to tell a soul. Even when she was an adult and knew that she could talk about what had happened, she chose not to because she knew that no one else would understand. It was just something that helped her to feel closer to him, and she didn't want to share.

She remembered an occasion when she was about 6 years old. He had decided to make her some pancakes after she declared that she was hungry and he said, "I tell you the recipe, but it's OUR secret!"

On another occasion, it was one of their numerous chess sessions. He was winning. He showed her exactly how he achieved every win. Once again, he told her that it was their secret, and only theirs, not to tell anyone. She felt like his accomplice. She felt important.

When she grew up, she found that those playful secrets were things that she still couldn't share with people, but perhaps their biggest secret was the one that held her together through the years. Preventing her from giving up her search.

She remembered that day clearly when he looked into her eyes and said,

"Listen, Lottie, if one day I won't be coming back, do not worry, I will always be somewhere in another house, maybe in another country, but always there for you," and that was their big secret.

That secret kept her going.

The hope of seeing him again kept her happy, no matter how many times she felt sad.

She marched through life like her grandad marched through those steep mountains. She kept his pace, his strength, his straight back, his wisdom.

But she struggled as she saw her family grieving for the man, and once or twice, she nearly said something.

"Don't cry, he will come back," she'd often say to other relatives, however with her only being 15, they assumed that was just her way of grieving, of dealing with it.

She was loyal to him, a loyalty that went well above the one that she gave to her own parents.

More loyal to him than she ever could be to herself.

With each new year, she wished for her grandfather to return home. As she grew older and started considering the possibility that he might be dead, she decided she would find him. If she did, indeed, discover that he had actually died, then at least she could get some closure and find out what really happened to him. Thing was, if she never at least tried to find out, she would just be broken-hearted forever.

If he had died at home, at least she would have had some kind of answers. Instead, inside her head, she was still a 15-year-old girl sitting by the window, just waiting for this man to return home.

She never allowed herself to believe anything had happened to him, but at some point, around her 30th birthday, the thought of letting it go crossed her mind. A part of her recognized it was the healthy thing to do. It was why she chose to leave Vienna and start all over in a new city, however as she stood in that room with that letter in her hand, all of the defenses that she had built around her questions had come crumbling down.

Mentally, she was exhausted, and she quite simply didn't know what to do anymore.

A body lacking happiness. Beautiful blue eyes that were lacking their sparkle.

A soul lost in a sea of tears.

2

"*People and things pass away, but not places.*"
-Daphne du Maurier

She stood there for several moments after her friend was gone, unsure of what to do now that she had what she wanted. She looked at the letter and proceeded to open it, her heartbeat increased with each second. When she finally pulled the letter out slowly, she stared at it, numbed. She looked into the envelope to see if she had missed anything. Then she looked around her to see if something had dropped. Nothing.

Laying her eyes on the words on the paper, she braced herself to read it.

Hotel Yalta

Prague

"In less than a week?" she said out loud.

What was she supposed to do with this? Was she supposed to pack up and just go to this place in Prague? Would he be waiting for her there? What was she going to do there exactly? See him? Bring him home? Why didn't he just come to find her?

She knew it wouldn't be the latter. He was too old. She smiled remembering the days when she was a little girl, and he would hold her hand and take her around the town wherever they needed to go. They especially loved to go to the bookshop, walking through the aisle and picking out books about plants. He loved plants, but she suspected that there was more to it than just the fact that he was a botanist. There was always a smell of plants, flowers, and herbs around him.

She had vivid memories of him from way before he left. Memories of those long times they spent in the gardens, in Vienna at the Belvedere, or just in the woods.

She couldn't stop playing all those scenes repeatedly in her head. Something was nagging at the back of her mind. As though she was trying to remember something. The more she tried to figure it out, the more it eluded her. So, she stopped trying and just focused on planning her unexpected trip.

"I'm sorry, Mitzi, we have barely moved in, and I already have to leave. You'll have to go spend some time with Ingrid, but, you know... she will look after you so well," she said, looking down at her dear companion.

For the first time in a long time, she was starting to entertain the idea that maybe it was time to let go and just live her life. The fact that this letter came at that exact time just made her weak. Because for the first time, she started thinking that everything might be fine. The note didn't answer any questions, though.

Nothing feasible could point her to clues as to whether or not he was alive and waiting, or if this was some sort of joke. She was scared that it would be the latter, but she couldn't bear to entertain the possibility that it would be the former, and her passing on the opportunity to see him again.

She wasn't a stranger to Prague.

She knew her way around the city because she had visited a few times. She knew she would be comfortable navigating the city, but the feeling of unease remained deep in her chest.

She started to imagine all the things she was going to tell him. So much had happened in the last fifteen years. So much had changed. She wanted to tell him all her achievements, make him proud. She wanted to tell him all about how his absence had changed her, changed the course of her life. She had so much to complain about, but perhaps more importantly, she had so much she wanted to ask him.

I cannot wait to hold your beautiful, trembling, always cold hands. I have so many things to tell you, she thought to herself as she cast a wistful glance in the direction of his picture that she had placed on her dresser. Her heart was bursting from euphoria. She was fighting the urge to cry, but she could barely hold herself together.

19th December

She stood outside Ingrid's door with a look of apprehension on her face. She had been friends with Ingrid for so long and had many conversation about this, but she felt that Ingrid didn't quite understand that this was a part of who she was.

She knew the facts. She had seen pictures of her grandad.

Yet, Ingrid had never been privy to how deeply her grandfather's disappearance affected her, and how much of her personality was built around that one event.

For Ingrid, and most other people who knew about her grandfather outside her immediate family, the man was just an old man who got confused, had lost his way, and never returned home. It was a sad story, but from their perspective, it was one that she ought to have gotten over already.

However, from her perspective, it was way more than a lost, older man.

It was a significant part of her childhood that just disappeared suddenly, for which she had never gotten closure. It was her life taking a wildly different turn than it would have taken if he had never disappeared. There were details to that fact that she just didn't share with people. She knew they wouldn't understand, but she also knew that it was just a matter of time before Ingrid insisted on understanding the whole story.

Before she could ring the bell, the door flung open, and Ingrid stood there, eyeing her warily.

"Are you coming in?"

Lottie smiled and followed her into the house without a word, Mitzi following them close behind.

Lottie looked at Ingrid with her eyes full of emotions, wanting to tell her, but knowing she couldn't. This was her best friend from childhood, someone with whom she had shared so much. So why was this one thing off-limits? Why couldn't she just say what needed to be said and allow her friend to offer her sympathies? Maybe even her help? But then, perhaps the sympathies were the exact thing she was trying to avoid.

"I'm sorry to bother you...but I need your help. Mitzi needs a place to stay for a while."

Ingrid glared at her, having already figured out that something was wrong without actually asking her. She could tell that Lottie was not in a good place, but she had always assumed she would be one of the first to know if her best friend ever needed help.

"Do you want to talk?"

Lottie met her eyes for the first time. A million emotions were running through her face at the same time as she said

"No, sorry... Not yet."

Ingrid nodded.

"Do you think you'll ever come around to talking about it?" She asked again.

"Eventually."

Ingrid looked down, a small smile curling her lip. That was good enough for her.

Perhaps what she needed was an assurance that they were still best friends no matter what. It wasn't just about the fact that Lottie wanted to handle what she was going through alone. Was Lottie in trouble? Did she need money?

"So, will you have Mitzi for a few days?" Lottie asked again, snapping her friend out of her thoughts.

"Yes, of course. You know you don't even have to ask that."

Lottie smiled. She knew she could always count on her. She rubbed Mitzi's head as she gave her a kiss before handing Ingrid the leash.

"I'll go get her toys and food in the taxi."

Her walk was suddenly interrupted...

"Do you need money? Or do you need anything at all?" asked Ingrid.

"You are a very good friend, but don't worry, I'll be safe.

I'll let you know soon enough what's going on, but for now, I need to just work it out for myself," Lottie explained, as she turned around without another word and returned to the taxi.

She had a journey ahead of her, and it was also a mental journey of seeing the man that had haunted her dreams for fifteen years.

Ingrid continued to stand at the door until Lottie's taxi was out of sight. Then, she wondered what the right thing to do would be. Should she call Lottie's parents and let them know that their daughter was acting strange? Or should she wait and trust her friend's judgment, hoping that she was indeed safe and sound?

"I guess we have to trust her," Ingrid said to Mitzi with a smile.

Lottie's mind raced:

"I cannot believe I'm finally going to see you," she thought as she picked up her luggage.

"I was right to believe you were out there. You were honest; you told me the truth and kept your promise, my dear grandad." as she got on the train.

"And I swear I never told anyone your secret, our secret!" were the last things she said as the train started to move.

Berlin −Prague 4 hours journey, she noticed on the timetable.

The sight of the train calmed her.

Finally, *finally*, she had something to look forward to, something to anticipate. Booking the train seat had been easy, the difficult part would be to sit still and allow the sound and movement of the train to put her in the kind of mind-frame that it always did.

She loved train rides.

Ever since she was a little girl, she had loved being on a train. It had a soothing effect on her, and her favorite part was when the train went through tunnels or long spans of grassland.

She remembered train rides with her grandfather. Usually, they would go to some famous garden or go on what they called a *Wildflower hunt*. These hunts traditionally comprised them going up on the Tyrol mountains and looking for rare or new species of gentian.

Those trips were also about having time with her grandfather. They were always about giving the memories that would last her a lifetime when he was gone. As the train gathered speed, she leaned back and closed her eyes. She set off a day before the note said to come. She just wanted to enjoy the sight of the city and maybe also clear her head before having to face her grandfather. *Then, something passed her, and her eyes snapped open. It was a man in a long black coat and a hat. She sat still, watching his back move through the coach, heading for the door.*

For a second, she thought it was him.

She remembered the times when he would hold her hand in that park they loved so much. Those moments she cherished so much. He was a funny, a bit eccentric old man who knew how to make her listen to his stories. She wiped a hand across her face and looked out the window. Everything took a while to come into focus. She still had a significantly long way to go.

Next to her sat a gentleman. He kept himself to himself, and she noticed he was reading a Czech newspaper. She knew only a few words of Czech. She wondered if her grandad was now fluent in this captivating language.

The carriage was buzzing with people, young and old. People returning home for Christmas to see their loved ones, and tourists to see the Christmas markets under a blanket of snow. Lottie smiled, noticing how easy it is now to cross borders compared to the past that her grandad described so well. She suddenly remembered a conversation her grandad had with her about Prague Spring.

He knew a lot.

She stared into the distance for a while, trying to put to words a million emotions that were running through her at that moment.

"What will you say to him when you see him?" she asked herself. "Where have you been?" she thought, then shook her head.

"No. That won't do. Where he's been is irrelevant. I am just glad that he's here now."

"Why didn't you come for me... or let me know you were okay?" But she knew that was no good either. While it would be nice to get some sort of explanation, she knew that this was not her priority.

She just wanted him back. She just wanted him back with her.

She thought about what his hug would feel like now. Would he pat her on the head like he always did, or would his arms be too frail to raise?

Resting her head on the window, Brno station disappeared behind her. The sky was holding a lot of snow, and she felt a sense of peace, happiness, and trepidation.

3

"You can crush the flowers, but you can't stop the spring"

-Pablo Neruda

Prague

She knew she could not afford the Yalta for her stay or that kind of hotel, especially considering the time she planned to spend in Prague.

She had spent most of her time on the train looking for alternative hotels that were much cheaper and within her budget. As the train slowly ground to a halt, she hastily made up her mind and decided which hotel to choose from the list she had made.

One thing that she planned on doing was exploring the city, especially since life had brought her to Prague again.

As she walked into her small, little dusky hotel room in Karlín district, she unloaded her travel bag and changed her clothes, slipping into a cozy pink roll-neck jumper as the windy evening made her shiver.

Then, she went walking down the street. She had always loved and wanted to do just that, just walking through the streets of Prague.

As she approached Charles Bridge and saw the water passing before her, she took in all the beauty of the river Vltava. Prague wouldn't be so romantic, mystical, and magical without the river. So, she stopped and just stared.

At this moment, she knew that the water, bridge, and whole environment were features in one of the stories her grandfather mentioned. She had previously visited Prague in summer, not winter. Hence, she never noticed that Prague in winter with the fog and mist, it looked at its best. It was like walking on the pages of a fairy-tale book.

She walked up to Prague castle, passed Kafka's house on Golden Lane, and came down those wide steps, surrounded by red roofs and yellow painted houses till Kampa.

It was a long walk, but it was just what she needed. It was almost as though she could hear her grandfather's voice in her head, telling her how important that city was to him and how she needed to pay close attention to the things around her.

Lottie treated herself to a nice meal in Křemencova. The restaurant was busy, and she loved all that chattering.

She avoided the crowded streets and passed little back roads on her way back to her hotel. She could only hear her steps on the cobbles, where cold, tiny snowflakes slowly came down from the deep blue sky. The moment she closed the hotel room door behind her, she sat on her bed, looking out.

He sat alone at the reading desk that everyone used. There was a thick leather-bound book open in front of him. He was writing something inside of it. There were many legends about that old leather-bound journal. The family thought it contained all the secrets of his life. Now the real question is, what was the secret of his life exactly? Many people could not answer this question. There were other theories, though some people believed that that book was something found on the floor when he was a boy. Not many people were sure exactly how the journal held importance to him. Apart from him, nobody else ever had it. So, there was no natural way to know what was in it, and they would come into his house with a faraway look whenever he was holding the book. Grandad had many secrets, and this day as she walked over to him writing in his book, she had no idea that she was about to become the only person who knew what was in the journal.

"Grandad, what are you writing?" She asked him with her innocent eyes staring up at him. He paused from his writing and looked at her. For a moment, it seemed like he would turn away or call someone to get her. But he did neither. Even though she could already read some words, she couldn't figure out the words that were written in her grandfather's old journal.

"I'm writing a nice story," he said.

"What's the story about?" she asked. He seemed to hesitate once again before he answered.

"It's about a young man who had to undergo a lot of suffering."

It was a good enough answer for a six-year-old. He didn't need to keep talking at that point, but he did, and she listened. The tale he told her that day made no sense.

But it was a good story because it ended happily. That happy ending was more than enough for her.

Presently, she found herself wondering whatever happened to the old journal her grandfather used to keep. Did someone inherit it? Did it get stolen, or did her grandfather hide it? Where was it?

Why was she remembering that old journal now?

She frowned as she tried to make sense of it. The old man was probably lying when he said he was writing a story. Her grandfather was never a writer. He was a botanist who loved plants and mostly talked to trees. He was not the man to go to for elaborate story writing. Maybe she was wrong, and maybe there was more to the man than she or his son knew; maybe she was about to find out.

20th December

As soon as she saw the first light of a shy sunrise, she sprung out of bed and began to get ready. It was going to be a long day, and the knowledge of that dictated how she dressed and what she decided to wear or not wear. Because she had developed a phobia that she would get there too late or that she would cry and mess up her face, she didn't wear makeup.

He should be eighty-six years old based on the age he left home and disappeared. That was an old age to be, and she was personally proud of him, but on the other hand, she was concerned knowing that he might have trouble recognizing people, especially if they looked different. So, she tried to look just like she did when he left. She pulled her blonde, long hair into a ponytail, making her look younger.

Stepping out onto the street from her hotel, she decided that the day was just fantastic enough for her to take a walk, and that was precisely what she did.

She walked from her hotel to Mustek Metro station and up nearly to the top of Wenceslas Square. Her heart started racing as she got closer.

There was a sweet, pleasant smell in the air of cinnamon and mulled wine.

The Yalta stood imposing and beautiful. She took a big breath because she had not been in that hotel before. It was beautiful from the outside and felt like a palace inside too. That day, its façade with that wintery light in the sky, with the snow starting to fall, it looked a pale shade of pink; sumptuous and glamorous with its gold and burgundy sofas.

She came early in the morning as the letter didn't specify the time. A quick look at the clock behind the reception desk told her that it was just 10 o'clock. She glanced around.

No one was there for her.

She looked frantically around her, waiting to see an old man with white hair. Her eyes were scanning the faces of everyone around, trying to locate the man she had come to see, but he was nowhere to be found.

"Where are you? I can't see you."

She muttered under her breath as she turned round and round.

She wanted to scream and probably shout, "GRANDAD, where are you, grandad?"

Her throat was hurting as she tried to keep calm while fighting tears.

She was distraught. It was as though something snapped within her. She had walked into that hall with high hopes and confidence in the future; now, all she felt was despair, anger, and pain.

All of which she thought she had successfully triumphed over.

Lots of people were leaving and others arriving in a whirlwind of luggage, bell boys, and noisy trolley wheels.

Midday came, and just as she was starting to turn around one last time, she felt a hand touching her shoulder. For a second, she froze.

They had touched her shoulder again, and she knew in that moment that it wasn't him.

"Yes?" She said as she spun around semi angrily.

She wasn't in the mood for unnecessary conversations.

The man that stood there was significantly younger than the old man she was expecting. He looked to be at twenty at the most. He was dressed in the hotel uniform.

"Miss Lottie?" he asked.

"Yes!"

The young receptionist handed her an envelope.

"For you, ma'am," he said.

She stared at the envelope and then at him for a moment.

"Who brought this? Was it an old man? Who brought this?" she asked him.

"I am sorry, I can't help you with that. I wasn't even on my shift when it came in.

I was instructed to make sure you get it," he said.

She glared at him as she received the envelope, trying to figure out what was happening for a moment. Tears were already gathering in her eyes, but she tried to fight them.

She sat down slowly on a far too low sofa. She opened the envelope and slipped out the note inside.

She glanced at the receptionist one more time and then at the envelope again, feeling increasingly unsettled because of what had just happened.

She had left her hotel room with anticipation of meeting her grandfather. Now she was being handed another letter.

What was she going to do with it?

She looked at the note, and all it had was an address in Teplice.

Teplice? She knew Teplice.

She had been there multiple times in the past. And yes, it was her grandfather who brought her there.

It was his hideout, and he said he had owned it for a very long time. He bought it shortly after getting married to the love of his life, her grandmother Zezilia.

This was another one of his secrets. Not even his son knew about it. When her grandfather had first gone missing, she had gone to Teplice a couple of times to

see if he was there, but he wasn't. It would have been too easy.

She had given up on Teplice when she found a new couple in the apartment and realized that her grandfather was most likely never coming back to that building even if he was still alive.

Now he wanted her to come to Teplice.

What was he doing back at the apartment he had sold... or rented out? She wasn't even sure. The couple had never actually told her that he had sold it to them. They just told her that they lived there now. Standing in the doorway that day, she felt like rushing in and chasing them out of the house. How dare they infiltrate her grandfather's house like that? It felt like a very personal space for her, and they were in it. It looked like they kept the place the same, but she didn't get a good look, so she wasn't sure.

She had gone home and cried for hours that day.

She wondered what her grandfather would think of strangers in his place.

Now that she thought about it, they seemed shifty.

She had noticed it, but she had put it down to their discomfort at having a stranger at their door asking for her missing grandfather for the third time.

She wasn't so sure anymore.

She found herself wondering what they were hiding.

She had questions, and this time, she wasn't about to let things slide. If her grandfather had written to her from that house or asked her to come to that house, she knew that somebody had lied to her, and she was going to make them talk.

She was at her wit's end now, and she would call the police if it became necessary.

She turned and walked out of that hotel lobby with a determined look. She was ready. The last fifteen years had culminated in this very moment.

This was it... she was going to get the answers once and for all.

4

"Everything that you love, you will eventually lose, but in the end, love will return in a different form."
-Franz Kafka

She whirled around and stepped out to find a taxi.

She would be going to Teplice where she had been as a child, and she had come there with her grandfather. At his place, she knew that if she concentrated well, she would remember what the apartment looked like inside. She knew that Teplice is a renowned spa town in the north of the Czech Republic at the border with Germany, an hour drive from Prague and nearly 5 hours from Vienna.

She must have been about only 10. On more than one occasion, they had gone to Teplice together. It started to feel like it was where he liked to go whenever he wanted to read or just have a quiet environment.

She remembered getting on the rather noisy train, and they had gone to Prague from Vienna, and then he drove to Teplice with a car he hired.

She vividly remembered the small apartment on the first floor of that beautiful light green walled building. The neat little room that served as the living room had a shelf containing what seemed like hundreds of books. When she started picking those books one after the other and reading them, it felt like a wonderful way to travel the world. Now that she was an adult, she often wondered if books were just something she shared with her grandfather. Or perhaps it was her way of getting close to him, even though he wasn't around anymore.

Her grandfather's house, his clothes and everything else that he touched, cigarettes and eucalyptus. Occasionally she could perceive the smell of lavender oil. And as old as he was, it would keep everywhere so tidy. There was never a bowl in the sink, or even a piece of dirt on the table. There was always some sort of flowers around this house; on the window sill outside, maybe even in his bedroom.

But perhaps what stood out to her in her childhood with her grandfather in Teplice was the park right across the street from his house, where they used to go.

She particularly loved going there because of the fountain that stood majestically at the center.

"Dobrý den", said the taxi driver whilst opening the car's door to Lottie.

As she got into the taxi in preparation to go to Teplice, she wondered if that fountain was still there. It had been so long, and she had not even thought about the fountain in the context of the park for a long time.

It was the summer holiday of 2002, and then he retook her in 2006, just a year before he left. Nobody knew where they were going. They were not trying to keep a secret or anything like that. It was more like they just didn't mention it to anyone. This was something that they had done a couple of times before. Perhaps, if she had known that this would be the last time they would travel together in that way, she would have paid much more attention.

She wrapped her arms around herself and adjusted herself in her seat as she looked out into the streets of Teplice.

She loved the open air, the fresh crispy wintry air. Days like this, long past, came floating into her mind. Yet, it felt like a thousand years ago now.

"This city is beautiful. I can see why Grandad would choose this city. He must have loved it here; but what is the significance of this town to him?"

I will find everything. I will know everything before I leave this town."

She remembered the old picture of her grandad that sat on her father's desk at home. In the picture, her grandfather had some old-school outfits on. A white shirt rolled up at the sleeves and grey trousers. He had a dark grey hat on and his usual cigarette in his hand. He looked like he was 35... maybe 40 at the time. She used to think as a little girl that her grandfather had been very handsome as a young man. He remained very handsome into his late sixties and right up until his wife, the love of his life, died. That was when the grief descended onto his face.

It was when she started catching him staring into the distance. He tried so hard to keep up appearances, but she could see that he was in pain.

"We are in Teplice, ma'am, where exactly do you want to go?"

It took several seconds for her to focus and realize exactly where she was. Then she slowly pulled herself into a full sitting position.

"Děkuji, I think I'll get off here and find my way."

She slowly started to remember part of the city.

Finding the park was quite easy, and even though she could see the house almost immediately, she decided to explore the park again.

She sat on a bench and suddenly she remembered all the secrets they shared.

She smiled, thinking how loud they laughed at his jokes and how silent they were when picking up flowers in the Alps.

He could have chosen to be like all of the other older people, but he just remained eccentric. Everyone knew him, and everyone respected him, but despite all that, he was kind and had a way of greeting everyone when they met on a trail, hiking.

"Grandad... why do you take your hat off when you greet people?" she asked once.

He looked at her with that amused yet endearing look.

"Because they all know me. I'm famous."

She just stood there and watched him talk. She believed everything, which allowed them to have a lot of fun.

As a grown woman, though, she realized that her grandfather had not been a star at all.

Neither had all those people known him. In reality, he was just a very polite man who liked greeting people as though he knew them from somewhere, and they greeted him back.

The smell of eucalyptus and arnica was always on his clothes, his hat, and his skin.

She remembered one day as they hung out in the house in Teplice together. He had suddenly stopped what he was doing and looked at her with those steady eyes. She knew instantly that he was about to say something serious, so she sat upright.

He said to her,

"I love you very much Lottie. So much that the very thought of not seeing you every day hurts me deep in my chest, but sometimes, we have to make some decisions and do some things that may be very easy to misunderstand. If and when that day comes for me, I want you to remember that I love you, and that I will never abandon you."

His eyes clouded with tears very briefly, and then he continued,

"i have lived a nice life. I had your father, and from him I got you, and I am so proud of all that".

Again, she nodded as though she understood, even though she didn't, and the whole conversation was so strange to her. It wasn't until she was grown that she realized how similar to a breakup speech her grandfather's speech had been that day.

"When I am gone, you will be tempted to search for me. If it makes you feel better, then perhaps you should do it, but don't let it consume you.

Also, don't come and stay in Teplice. I most likely won't be here," he said.

She became confused, but she nodded.

"And know that whenever you miss me, I'll be missing you too."

"Yes, grandpa."

That had been just a few weeks before that hiking trip. It was as though he knew that something would happen to him.

Now that she looked back on it, she was pretty sure that he knew, and for some reason, she just knew to go to the house he had told her not to go to.

Snapping out of her memories, she stopped in front of the building in U Hadích lázní. It looked the same, mostly. The carved sculptured flowers under each window were still there.

For a moment, she wanted to call her parents. She wanted to tell them everything and just have someone to support her, but she soon remembered that no one knew about the letter and all the secrets that her grandfather had kept with her.

She sighed silently as she realized that she had to handle everything on her own.

The entrance remained the same, a big strong oak door. It smelt spicy, and she didn't even have to come too close to perceive that smell.

As she stood there, she realized that her grandfather probably told her another of his tales.

It looked like he never really left Teplice. She walked in and through the narrow corridor. The letter remained clutched in her hand as she took a deep breath and tried to regain some of her composure.

She was just about to knock at the apartment when the door opened, and someone stepped out. She stood there, just staring at the person who had emerged from her grandfather's apartment. It was a dark haired woman who looked to be about 40 years old.

"Good afternoon, my name is...." but she didn't finish because the woman looked her in the eyes and smiled.

"Lottie? It's so nice to meet you again."

Lottie was shocked that the woman knew her name. She tried to remember if they had met before, but there was no memory of such a meeting in her mind.

"Lottie?" the woman repeated.

She snapped out of her thoughts.

She silently looked around, almost wildly, subconsciously waiting for her grandfather to step out of a corner somewhere.

That didn't happen.

"Please, Lottie, come inside." The lady said with that gentle smile again.

Lottie followed her into the house. She was right in her suspicion. The house looked almost the same. Those pale green walls hadn't been touched. She looked around and instantly got flooded with memories. She could see herself sitting with her grandfather and playing cards in that same room. She could hear his laughter as he won every round.

She looked around for somewhere to sit.

"Where is my grandfather?" she asked. The lady looked at her.

"Where is he?"

This time Lottie glared at the woman as though accusing her of something.

She pressed her lips together to prevent herself from saying something nasty.

Right at that moment, the door from the inner room opened, and a man stepped out. He looked like he was in his early 50s. He was tall, pale-skinned, blond, with blue eyes and a mustache belonging to the 70s. Or at least that's what Lottie thought.

"Lottie. My name is Milan, and this is my wife, Zora" the man said.

Lottie looked at him with weary eyes.

"Who are you?" she asked him as she looked at the two of them.

She glared at him for a few seconds, and then she suddenly understood what was happening. The combination of all her movements until the moment she got to the apartment in the town suddenly made sense to her. She should have suspected it, but there was a tiny bit of her that hoped.

She took an intense breath and looked into his eyes with all the seriousness she could gather without breaking down into tears.

"Just tell me the truth. My grandfather is dead, isn't he?" and even as she asked, there was a bit of hope in her heart that he would say no.

The man didn't have to say much. His eyes confirmed her worst fears long before his lips did.

"Yes, he died last year."

She took a deep, sharp breath and looked away from him.

She started nodding her head, staring at one corner of the room because she was trying to control herself and not burst into tears.

It didn't help her very much that she was inside the apartment she grew up loving and caring about. After moments of taking deep breaths and calming herself, she turned her head back and looked at the man.

"So, what is this then? Why am I here?"

Milan started to open his mouth to say something, but she cut him off.

"Is this some sort of joke or something?"

Neither of them responded. They could feel her pain and knew that it was best to let her express her thoughts.

"You waited for him to die before calling me. Why now? Why are you talking to me about him now?" Her voice carried all the emotions of the past years even though her eyes refused to shed a tear.

"We would have called you much earlier. We didn't call you because he didn't want you to see him like that," he explained.

She nervously, sarcastically laughed.

"Your grandad Johann, my uncle, loved you, loved us very much. He just could not bear for you to see him as anything other than your strong, powerful grandfather," Milan added.

Lottie couldn't bring herself to believe him, but he continued talking.

"Besides, he didn't just leave you. He had important things to do."

"Wait a moment. You said your uncle?" Lottie interrupted.

"Yes, Lottie. The people who raised your grandfather had another son. A little boy that was born when your grandfather was already an adult. That son was my father. They were born in

Teplice, hence why the town was full of meaning for him and why he returned."

"And what other important things did he have to do that required him to leave me? For 15 years?"

She could feel the sadness rise up into her throat as she grew more and more unable to hide it.

He sat closer to the edge of his chair and said to her in a very controlled voice,

"Listen very closely, Lottie. Your grandfather did not abandon you."

Unable to control herself, she wrapped her arms around herself and started to cry.

It was a deep sound of a broken heart.

"Why didn't he let me see him? I spent all of my years as an adult thinking that he just left me."

The emotions were so high that she started to shake.

Milan looked over to Zora, before he walked over to Lottie and wrapped his arms around her shoulders.

"Lottie...your grandfather cared for you very deeply, but he also had to stay out of sight.

There were things about him that you did not know, things that affected him right from when he was a child into adulthood. Even though he was your beautiful, amazing grandfather, he had also been a young man and, before that, a boy."

That just puzzled her, it didn't even make sense in the context of the situation. How was that relevant?

She disengaged herself from him, and he went over to his chair to sit down.

"What are you talking about right now, Milan?" she asked through her tears, almost in frustration.

"Lottie, I will explain everything.

I am talking about the fact that your grandfather was a part of the reformists of 1968. And so was his wife. That was how they met. They attended a couple of meetings together, and their love blossomed."

Lottie sat still, staring at him with a look in her eyes that told him that she believed him and disbelieved him almost at the same time.

What did this man mean by her grandfather was a reformist?

All the years she had known him, she couldn't remember ever hearing him talk about politics. He was a simple man, in a way that did not involve meddling with politics. He never showed interest in political issues, nor did he attend rallies or meetings.

How could he have been an activist? She shook her head from side to side.

"So why didn't we know this of him?" she asked with a confused look on her face.

It was quickly becoming apparent to her that there were many things she didn't know about her grandfather. She felt left out of what she thought she knew about their secrets.

The more she tried to deny what was being said to her, the more it made sense.

"After the invasion and after Dubček was arrested, many of the elites of the time fled the country. Thousands of them would end up in different parts of Europe and America. That's when your grandfather left for Vienna, like most of the intellectuals, such as journalists, writers, artists, and musicians did.

Around that time, your grandmother found out that she was pregnant. He realized that he had just one thing to do at that point. He had to protect his wife and unborn child."

Lottie sat expressionless listening to what Milan was saying. The sea of questions flooded her mind, stopping her from truly processing anything that was being said.

"He wanted to die close to home and the things that he loved," he continued before he paused and looked at her intensely. Then he gestured towards the bookshelf.

"This shelf full of books would have been enough to get him arrested in those days.

It would have been enough for him not to see the light of day for a very long time.

I think he just wanted to feel like he was in control of his own life for once."

By the time Milan was done talking, Lottie was deeply in tears.

Multiple things started to come together for her.

It seemed like her grandfather couldn't sleep with his eyes closed. Looking back, she remembered how he was always on alert, and the slightest of sounds would wake him up. He was always on guard. Even though the man smiled, they rarely ever talked about his past, and, when he did, it was just to mention the fact that he had known her grandma for a very long time. There was barely any time for her to ask serious questions about his life. Questions about his youth and what he was up to. With him there was always something to do or somewhere to go.

"As they started to grow older, he missed the life he had as a young man. He realized that the one thing he wanted to be more than any other thing was the person he was when his country was free, before that invasion of August."

Lottie sat there in that chair, listening to every word.

"Why didn't my father know of all this?" she asked and wondered how her father, his son, didn't know anything about it.

"I'm not sure why he didn't tell his son or the rest of his family about my dad and me, however I know he had his reasons. Most certainly to protect them, to protect you."

As the tears subsided, she calmed herself down and looked into Milan's eyes.

He walked over to the bookshelf and pulled a folder off the top of the shelf, dropping it gently into her lap.

She touched it lightly and then looked up at him from her sitting position.

"What is this?" she asked.

"Open it." At this point, Zora, Milan's wife, looked up.

Lottie looked at the envelope and opened it. It was a whole file of sheets of paper. On closer inspection, she noticed the heading and instantly figured out what it was.

"No..." she exclaimed.

"Yes," Milan said in affirmation.

She stood up, paced the room for a bit, and walked back to her chair.

"What was he thinking?" she asked out loud. The question was directed at no one in particular, but Zora answered all the same.

"That he loved you. He wanted to make sure that you will be OK. So, he was thinking of you the whole time."

Lottie looked down at the documents in her hands, and her hands started to shake.

"Are you trying to tell me that I own this house now?"

Milan smiled.

"You haven't gone through all the papers. There is more," he said.

Her heart started to pound very loudly as she went through each document, one after the other. Even though she wasn't paying attention anymore, he continued talking to her in the background.

"We have lived here near your grandfather for almost 15 years now. Lottie, there are many clues around the house on what grandfather wants you to do. Take some time. The house is yours."

She was taken aback by all this.

"I still cannot believe I will never see him again, hold hands again."

She said as she wiped the tears away from her eyes with her hands.

Milan clutched his hands together and avoided eye contact for a moment. He then briefly touched his chest.

Milan gently took Lottie's hand and placed it with a slow movement on his chest.

She was surprised.

He pressed his right hand on top of hers.

She felt his heartbeat, but she didn't understand what he was trying to say.

"You can feel his heartbeat. His heart still beats in here."

Now, even more distraught, she was unable to believe what he was saying to her.

"What do you mean, Milan? Please. Please explain to me."

He didn't answer her for a few moments. Suddenly her brows raised in realization.

"Are you telling me that you have my grandfather's heart?"

"Yes. I am living only because his heart is beating within me."

At that moment, he stood and slowly removed his shirt for her to see the scar.

She glared at him.

"Thank you..." she said, her mixed emotions evident in her voice.

It sounded more like a whisper—a mixture of disbelief and shock.

"Towards the end of your grandfather's stay with us, I developed a severe heart problem. I needed a new heart. Your grandfather took that sentence from the doctor thoughtfully. I remember he made a joke that he could give me his heart. We all laughed. Then, a few months after that conversation, one night, he called me saying he didn't feel well. The next morning things deteriorated quickly, and the very same afternoon, he was gone. Lottie...he was gone".

Milan was crying, too, now.

"We were both shocked. The doctor showed me the card your granddad had in his pocket.

He had a plan. The plan was clear and straightforward. He wanted me to have his heart, so he put me down as the beneficiary and recipient of that heart, which was in good condition, if no one else was to be found as a donor in the meantime. They told me that I had just a few hours to decide, so I had to make a decision.

It was that same day that we did my surgery. My dear uncle wanted me to have his heart, and that was what I did.

I didn't contact you immediately because I had a long way to recover, and more importantly, I couldn't find the courage.

How was I to face you and tell you all this?"

He paused and looked into her eyes again.

The room went quiet, silent, as Lottie sat there staring at Milan talking.

"It was in grandfather's character to offer his heart to people," she thought.

"He had a letter ready for you, the letter I sent you," Milan continued. "Your grandfather wanted to meet you one last time. Life decided otherwise."

Milan and his wife thought to give Lottie some space and time, perhaps to reflect on what has been a day full of emotions. They left her in the room and explained that it would be best for her to have some time alone to process everything.

Now alone, Lottie stood up slowly, walked over to the bookcase, and slipped the documents between books. Then she walked out of the house and toward the park.

She sat on the bench with tears streaming down her face as she finally allowed herself to feel the grief and gratitude to her grandfather. She had always known that he loved his family, he loved her, but she had never really understood what made him the way he was. She then walked to the botanical gardens she had always visited with her grandfather as a child. It was the place she could be alone with her thoughts of him. She walked through the garden, allowing the smell of plants to overwhelm her senses. This was as close as she could get to him without interruption, and she intended to take advantage of it. So, she stood in front of a row of linden trees.

Teplice wasn't only a geographical location where a letter came from.

It was her past, and from now on was also her future.

Their secret was safe, forever.

5

January, Berlin

Ingrid pulled the door open, expecting to see the delivery man she was waiting for. Instead, it was Lottie standing there, with a glow in her eyes that told Ingrid that whatever was happening with her was now over.

"Lottie!" she exclaimed.

"Ingrid!" she replied as the two of them hugged each other.

A small bark from inside the house told them that Mitzi knew that she was there.

Ingrid stepped back, and the dog jumped into her human's arms.

"Oh Mitzi, I've missed you so much!" Lottie said as she hugged and kissed her, and she returned the affection with her wet slobbering kisses.

Then, finally, she looked up at Ingrid.

"Was she a good dog?" she asked, eyeing Mitzi affectionately.

"She missed you!" Ingrid replied.

"I can see that. Thank you for having her."

"Don't thank me, come tell me everything," Ingrid said as she took Lottie's carry-on bag and walked into the house.

Again, Lottie sighed, but this time, it was not filled with sadness. It was a sigh of happiness and relief.

"Do you remember what I told you about my grandfather?" Lottie asked.

"Yes ... yes... you said he had gone missing while hiking."

"Yes... well... something happened."

"You found him?" Ingrid's eyes lighted up with excitement.

"Well, yes... kind of..."

"What do you mean, kind of? It's either you found him or...." Ingrid didn't finish the sentence as realization dawned on her at that exact moment.

"You found him, but he is ...."

"Yes... he is dead."

"Oh, no!" Ingrid said with her face showing how sorry she was to hear that.

"It's okay. I'm okay now."

"Are you sure?"

"Yes... yes, I am sure."

"Well, in that case, come tell me all about it, and don't leave anything out."

"So here is what happened. Do you remember when we were supposed to have an early lunch together, but I cancelled..."

"... and later showed up and asked me to sit Mitzi? Of course, I do," Ingrid said as if she wanted to fast forward Lottie's story.

"Well, that was the morning I received the first letter."

Ingrid was surprised as Lottie started to tell her what had happened.

She sat still as Lottie started to tell her everything. Her voice was steady as she recollected every single detail of what had happened to her since that fateful morning. Ingrid listened with rapt attention, and by the time Lottie was done talking, her eyes were filled with tears.

"Why didn't you call me? So you didn't have to go through all of that alone," Ingrid said to her friend.

"Well, I didn't even know if he was alive or gone at first and when I found out, it was already the end, and I just had too much to process at that point. So, I wanted to be alone," Ingrid nodded. She understood.

"That's okay. I just wish I were there for you, though," she said.

"You were. You looked after Mitzi. That was a huge part of why I could make the trip. So, thank you."

That evening, the two of them sat down and Lottie explained everything to Ingrid, sparing no details. She shared how she felt and told her all about Milan and Zora and everything she had found.

She found it liberating being able to share the truth for once. Even just saying it all out loud, she felt so much lighter, as if she could finally share what had actually happened with someone instead of the unknown being like a dark cloud over her head.

February, Teplice

She pulled the last boxes in with exhaustion written all over each movement however, even though she was tired, she felt very peaceful.

The house had been cleaned, but she had retained nearly everything. The rooms remained the same, and even the flowerpots stayed in their places. She loved it just so. She had never felt so much peace and happiness in all her adult years. It was as though all the questions she could ever have had been answered.

She sat gently on the bed in the room that had been her grandfather's. It was a room with large bay windows. She liked the way the sun spilled into the room and how she could roll the blinds and keep it all out if she wanted. With her feet still on the floor, she leaned back into the bed and closed her eyes. For a moment, she felt as though everything was back to those days when they were just visiting Teplice.

It was not just about the building. It was about everything else that was in it.

It was about the décor, the books, and the plants. It was about the structure and the ambiance of the place.

It was about that sweet smell of eucalyptus and cigarettes mixed with a delicate scent of lavender.

Mitzi would come to join her in a few weeks. She wanted to settle in first and get herself acquainted with her new home. The landlord of her former house was shocked when she informed him that she would be moving. He didn't understand, but he didn't pry. She didn't offer any explanations either. If he had paid attention, he would have noticed that she was highly radiant, happy even that she walked with a different kind of spring in her strides and a smile on her face.

He would have noticed that she was a different person.

Evening came, the streets were covered in snow. She lay down all dressed as she was. She just kicked her shoes off and with her arms crossed she stared at the ceiling, imagining her grandad looking at the same pale white ceiling. She looked at the bedside table on her left and opened the top drawer. Inside she saw what looked like a brown leather journal. She gasped. Her breath caught in her throat as she tried to calm herself down.

"It can't be," she thought.

But she was quickly learning not to take things for granted anymore. This book looked like her grandfather's old journal. What else could it be? She picked it up and brought it to sit on the couch. On opening the first page, she saw that elegant handwriting once again.

"To my beloved Lottie, this is the total of what I didn't get the chance or the courage to teach you.

But I hope that it brings you the fulfillment it brought me."

The words immediately brought tears to her eyes while holding the book in her hand. She realized that it was never the fear of her grandfather dying that kept her from moving on. Death was universal, and she had come to accept that as soon as she could understand the concept of it. Instead, it was the idea that her grandfather, her closest friend in the world, could leave her and disappear forever.

Holding that book in her hand brought everything into perspective for her. If she had any doubt about the reality of what was going on with her before, all of it was gone in that moment.

She opened to the next page.

He had this book since he was a child, and nobody had ever seen the inside of it.

She had never even thought that she would find it for one second. She assumed it was some sort of diary and that it was personal.

She was right about the latter. What she was not right about was that she would never see the inside

of it. She remembered something he had said to her once when they were hiking together.

Those words started to get meaning as she read each page of her grandfather's diary.

He had a lot to say about many things, from the events of 1968 to those that happened shortly after. Most of his writing was short and sharp, with just a few sentences of his own opinion. As she read those pages, she saw the political aspect of her grandfather.

It was like walking into a political meeting with one man doing all the talking.

She felt dizzy from all the information. The sheer amount of references stunned her.

As she felt herself getting lost in the words, she suddenly realized her door was unlocked, and she walked over and locked it. She needed to have an utterly uninterrupted time with the book. She soon got comfortable with the book's contents and just read for information and entertainment to feel closer to her grandfather through his handwriting, until she opened a page where everything was different. The words on that page were not political.

They weren't even stories or memories like any of the other pages. Instead, it was a detailed description of a distilling process. She could see the ingredients, the process, and the pieces of equipment. There was no doubt about it; she was looking at a formula for a liquor or a kind of syrup.

Something was rippling through her that she could barely contain. She waltzed back to the bookshelf and stood in front of it, looking at the title of each book.

She wasn't particularly looking for something to read, she was simply wondering what else she had missed. Was there something else in that house that she needed to see?

She was excited. So much so that she went back to the journal and continued reading through it. Some of the writings, she understood. Some she didn't, but as she started to approach the last page of the book, she found a folded piece of paper in there.

It was old and slightly stained but was otherwise in good condition. She indulged herself in the reading of everything she was finding. For the first time in years, she felt close to her grandfather.

She could barely sleep that night. Her mind raced and span from all the information she had learned that day. The mix of emotions wrapped themselves around her mind, the excitement of getting her answers keeping her awake. She finally got exactly what she wanted. It wasn't in the format that she was expecting, but underneath her insomnia lay a happiness that could only come from finding something that one had been searching for years. She was finally happy, content.

As soon as the old watch showed 9 o'clock the following morning, she stood up and reached over to the hook near the door, where she retrieved her coat and gloves, and headed out of the house to get some of the ingredients. If it came from her grandfather, she knew it was worth exploring, and she would waste no time doing just that. She had no idea that her life was about to change forever.

As she gathered the items on her list, a thought came to her mind. She knew she could not do her experiment alone.

"Milan!" she said under her breath and smiled, realizing she now had someone she could rely on who was local, too.

Even though her grandfather was gone, she knew she could count on them, and that was what she was going to do.

6

"To adopt a Country, you must first understand it."
- Vladimir Fedorovski

The trees waved lazily. The sweet colors of spring fading off them were almost unnoticeable. From time to time, the breeze would bring towards her the aroma of wine, rum, and different nectars pulled and cultured from various plants around the world. Each time this would happen. A small, familiar smile would grow on her face. Looking back, she almost couldn't believe that it had been five years since she planted her first linden trees in her garden.

Milan had been supportive, and so had his wife however what she enjoyed was not just the support; it was also the love of the family and the respect of strangers.

"Hey, my sweet Mitzi!" She sat down gently. She slid to the floor of the balcony beside her, admiring their beautiful garden. She was growing old. Mitzi was now in late dog adulthood, and she could tell she had just a few more years with her. She understood now that death was not always separation. It had been six years since her grandfather died and she didn't feel separated from him. She stayed close to him, and he stayed close to her too. The house in Teplice remained her permanent home.

The old grandfather's rocking chair was where she liked to sit with newspapers in the mornings. Even though everyone got their news off the internet now, she still wanted to sit with a cup of tea and the day's papers, going through the pages at her pace.

Mitzi settled in well in her new life. Ingrid was often visiting. Lottie signed up to learn Czech and the history of her country.

Lottie's liquor, made mainly with Gentian flowers and roots, was selling very well. After having found the ingredients on her grandfather's list, she realized she could make batches of them and make some profit. So that's exactly what she did. It was a way to spread and share her appreciation of her grandfather.

Her parents were also extremely proud of her success nevertheless were still wondering what made Lottie move to a small town in the Czech Republic.

This was her life, and it was the life she had always wanted, only better and far beyond her imagination.

Epilogue

Mitzi passed on that same winter. It was a freezing cold night and Lottie sat on the floor by her side, with tears running down her face. She kept her warm with the blanket wrapped around her but more intensely wrapped around the dog was all of her love. She knew she would never be the same again. She had had Mitzi for so long that she had become a part of her life.

Mitzi was the closest family member she had and now she was gone.

Because the house suddenly felt weird and empty, Lottie decided to do some renovations. She really just wanted to make the place fully hers and keeping busy helped her coping with the immense loss.

Three days into those renovations, she had some of the floor pulled out for repair and change and right under those hardwood floors, she came face to face with something that sent surprise and awe rushing through her. She went to her bedroom, slowly sat on the bed and immediately called Ingrid.

"I just found something incredible under the hardwood floor in the living room," she said.

Ingrid didn't ask what it was. If Lottie wanted to say what it was on the phone, she would have done exactly that.

"I'll come, I'll see you soon," knowing that her best friend needed her at that moment.

"The house is a mess. Wait 'till I call you," Lottie said.

Ingrid agreed and waited for her call.

A week went by without a call and Ingrid grew worried with each day.

"Call or not, I am going to see Lottie," she thought to herself.

So, that's exactly what she did. She went over to Lottie's and knocked on the door. The door opened and there stood Milan with two envelopes and a look of utter disbelieve in his eyes.

"Lottie's left," Milan said before turning back to walk into the fully renovated and well-organized living room.

"What do you mean Lottie left? When is she coming back?"

"I don't know."

There was a pause as Ingrid took the information in.

"Is she coming back?"

"I don't know."

Ingrid stood still, watching the letters in his hand. What Milan handed to her was really a comprehensive to-do list for Ingrid and Milan.

"It says that her parents will get a letter from Teplice, too," Milan said. It was clear to Ingrid that Milan was as confused as she was.

She nodded, for lack of anything better to do. She felt tired. They weren't prepared for this... nobody was.

"What are your thoughts, Milan?" asked Ingrid.

"My thoughts are...history is repeating itself," Milan replied with a look of slight concern on his face.

Inside the spotless apartment, everything was still there. Flowers, plant pots, books.

Lottie was already far. Alone with her secrets.

Of the same author

GLOOMY SUMMER 2022

Printed in Great Britain
by Amazon

11248073R00068